Little Wolf's

HANDY Book of

Poems

First American Edition published in 2002 by First Avenue Editions

Text copyright © 2002 by Ian Whybrow
Illustrations copyright © 2002 by Tony Ross

Published by arrangement with HarperCollins Publishers Ltd, London, England.
Originally published in English by HaperCollins Publishers Ltd under the title
LITTLE WOLF'S HANDY BOOK OF PEOMS

First Avenue Editions
An imprint of Lerner Publishing Group
241 First Avenue North
Minneapolis, MN 55401 U.S.A.

Website address: www.lernerbooks.com

Library of Congress Cataloging-in-Publication Data

Whybrow, Ian.
Little Wolf's handy book of poems / by Ian Whybrow ; illustrated by Tony Ross.
p. cm.
Summary: Little Wolf, in a series of letters to his parents, tries his hand at writing poetry and
produces some work that his friends admire and his parents find very useful.
ISBN: 0-87614-927-1 (pbk. : alk. paper)
[1. Wolves—Fiction. 2. Poetry—Fiction. 3. Letters—Fiction.] I. Ross, Tony, ill. II. Title.
PZ7.W6225 Li 2002
[Fic]—dc21
2002001743

Manufactured in the United States of America
1 2 3 4 5 6 – SB – 07 06 05 04 03 02

Little Wolf's HANDY Book of Poems

Ian Whybrow

Illustrated by Tony Ross

First Avenue Editions, Minneapolis

With love to Valérie and Judith

Private Place, the nettly end of the garden, Frettnin Forest, Beastshire.

Dear Mom and Dad, this is not a letter,
This is a poem (they are funner and better).
You say you hate poems, but I have done a lot,
Sum are a bit silly, but this wun hits the spot.
Also I have done sum nice wuns about you and Dad,
So come on, have a quick read, or I will get sad.
Yours rimbling rumbling rhyming-lee, from
Little Wolf, your Number 1 cub-bee.

P.S. Can you send a letter saying
Smellybreff, no drinking Little's
ink or else?

Private Place, the nettly end of the garden, Frettnin Forest, Beastshire.

Dear Mom and Dad,

Thank you for your fierce letter, it made me jump. You say give up riting poems, you are wasting your time. Also you say, what are they? Will they let down the terrible name of Wolf?

Answer: no, they are smart and proud things. Plus they are handy if you want to say something 'specially. Like Dad, if you get a sting, you can say:

> Gurr that bee,
> The crazy thing stinged me.
> Oo ah ow ee!

B z z z z z ν ν ν ν ν ν z z z

Handy, right?

Tell you what, I will do you a batch. See if you change your mind. I will start with some tips to help you like them. Ready?

Yours tipfully,

TIPS ABOUT POEMS

poems ought to

Poems ought to jump about,
At least I think they ought.
Most of the time, they're s'posed to rhyme,
Plus, try to keep them short.
The end.

how poems like getting read

When you read a poem,
Do not gulp it like a stew.
Give it a nibble like a flea,
Before you start to chew.

Also do not try to read
A ton of them at wun go.
Just read a couple at a time,
Or your brane will say, "Oh no!"

Plus when you write a poem
It makes you very proud.
So do not read them in your head,
They like getting read OUT LOUD.

My best letter for poems

S is my
best letter,
it is wiggly
like a snake.
But if you
do a lot of them,
it makes you
sort of ache.

I don't know
many poems
about the
letter S.
This might
be the only wun,
but that is just
a guess.

I will do an
achy sentence,
fishes
misses
kisses.
Plus, here
is another wun.
Sossiges
are delishus.

(Ow, my arm. I do not know Y I did that.)

But no tip for Smells

Smells is a hopeless riter,
But he likes getting inky.
If I do not hide my ink bottle,
He has a little drinky.

It is just a waste of time
Giving him poem tips.
His idea of riting poems
Is making a mess with his lips.

MY FAMILY
(you will like these I bet)

poem for Grizzle, my wolfie mom

Who taught me how to scratch and fight?
My mom.
Who showed me how a cub should bite?
My mom.

Who taught me badness in my crib?
Who taught me how to cheat and fib?
Who taught me never to DYB DOB DYB?
(Sob) My mom.

poem for Gripper, my wolfie dad
(But not Uncle Bigbad though)

Dad, you look like Uncle,
Only much fiercier.
Your eyes are not so close together,
But they are a lot piercier.

If wun of you was going
To make me into stew,
I think I would much rather
Get eaten up by you.

My bad uncle (M.I.P.)

Bigbad was my uncle,
He was very fierce and tall.
And if you asked him kwestions,
It drove him up the wall.

Like, "Uncle, you know your trousers
With holes all over the back?
Is that so we don't have to guess
If your shorts are white or black?"

Like, "Uncle, when you were little,
Did you have an axi-dent?
Did you keep falling on your face?
Is that Y it is so bent?"

Like, "Uncle, you said you hate spinach?
Do you know the stuff I mean?
That skwished-up, smelly, slimy stuff.
So why are your teef so green?"

But now he is a ghostie,
Bigbad is dead at last.
So all he does is Moan in Peace,
Serves him right for eating beans too fast.

If you ask him ghostie kwestions,
It still drives him up the wall.
And that is Y he bongs my head,
Not fair, I am only small.

Baby bro Smellybreff

Smells is such a miser,
And if he gets sum gold,
He tucks it up and kisses it,
Saying, "Night night, don't get cold."

His brane is even smaller
Than the smallest little wrinkle.
That is Y his bestest noise
Is money going chinkle.

Plus, when my dad made Smellybreff
A garage with a key,
He locked up all my dinky cars,
Saying "Nah Nah, Har Har Hee."

Smells in the bathroom

Smells is in the bathroom
Getting undressed.
This is the bit that
He likes the best.

Eating all the toothpaste,
Skweezing the shampoo,
Collecting all the bath toys,
And dropping them down the loo.

loo!

Smells the yo-yo bro

I like to see a yo-yo
On a little bit of string.
I like to whizz a walk the dog
And get a proper swing.

But I hate playing yo-yos
With my bruvver in the yard.
He swings his yo-yo all around,
And he always hits me hard.

That is how annoying
Our Smellybreff can get.
So how come he is always
Mom's darling baby pet?

Our lair

Our lair is very cozy,
Plus it is nice and smelly.
It's nice for hibernaters,
Because you can watch the telly.

It is better than a burrow hole
Or a bird box or a tent.
Normus Bear says dens are good,
But I have not tried dens yet.

I wunce had a look in a wasps' nest,
But that was 2 buzzy for me.
No, I like Our Lair! I do, so there!
Hip hip arrroooo times 3.

MY FRIENDS

Guess who?

My friend S wears a Go Crow hat,
He has never been a weasel or a shark.
He does not bite or skweek,
But he has a clever beak.
And he does not say a lot, only Ark!
His name is…?

Now this wun

His name is like a color,
(The same color as his fuzz).
He is also very noisy,
He is my best friend and cuz.
His name is…?

one more

He is strong and also scary,
He likes bashing people in.
He is big and nice and hairy,
But not horrible and thin.
His name is…?

(xtra Clue)

He is not Uncle Bigbad.
He is not a fat pear.
So I will give you wun more chance.
His name is…?
(So eeeeeesy!)

Stubbs Crow, Yeller, Normus Bear

22

HAVING ADVENTURES

Adventures was its name

There was a time
When I was small
I did not care for
Bangs at all.

And my friend Yeller
Long ago,
Got the trembles
In the snow.

My friend Stubbs,
I don't know Y,
Wunce was much 2
Scared 2 fly.

But then we had a sumthing,
Like a scary sort of a game.
And then we all liked being scared—
Adventures was its name.

what to go by on adventures

If you have just normal fun,
You go by a scooter or a bike.
But if you have adventures,
You can go by anything you like.

Wunce I went by crocodile,

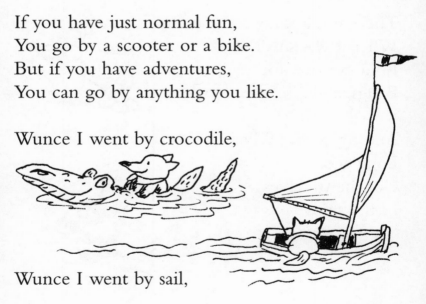

Wunce I went by sail,

Wunce I went by snowmobile,

Wunce I went by whale.

Wunce I went by picnic plates,
Skating on sum ice.

But my best way was by Stubby Crow,
Hmmm, yes, nice.

Zipwire adventures

Zipwires are funny
They are not like normal wire.

You get a nice shock going down
Then they bounce you off a tire.

My flying adventure

I have a friend called Stubby Crow.
Sumtimes he sits on wire,
And if he feels like it,
He can go up even higher.

Sum people fly in an air balloon
Or a blown-up rubber glove.
But Stubbs just does a flippy flap,
And up he goes above.

I wunce flew off a lamp post,
But I could not get the trick.
I found the air was a bit 2 thin,
And the ground was a bit 2 thick.
Bonk.

Kind of an adventure poem but more muckabouty

Normus brought his BEACH in a bag
His BEACH in a bag
His BEACH in a bag.
Normus brought his BEACH in a bag and
FLOPPED it on the floor. (PLONK)

Stubbs came along with his SEA in a pan
His SEA in a pan
His SEA in a SAUCEpan.
Stubbs came along with his SEA in a pan and
He began to pour. (SLOSH!)

Yeller brought his BUCKET and spade
His BUCKET and spade
His BUCKET and spade.
Yeller brought his BUCKET and spade and
SAT down on the shore. (PAT PAT PAT PAT)

I counted up all the LITTLE sand pies
All the LITTLE sand pies
All the LITTLE sand pies.
I counted up all the LITTLE sand pies
Going 1-2-3-5-4!

Then—
Smells came along and JUMPED on the pies
He JUMPED on the pies
He JUMPED on the pies.
Smells came along and JUMPED on the pies...

That's why his bottom is sore! (OUCH!)

SNACKY POEMS

Bakebean bangs

I love bakebeans,
They are delish!
I am most happy,
When they are in my dish.

They are sweet and saucy,
 (Hem hem, a bit like me).
You can get them canteen size,
So handy 4 your tea.

Best to eat them with a spoon,
But never with a spade.
If you do, then ask your mom
To call the fire brigade.

Remember Uncle Bigbad went
Chomp Chomp and could not stop?
He got the Jumping Beanbangs,
And then he went off—POP!

So when you eat your bakebeans,
Make sure that they get chewed.
Or you might go bang at the table,
(Funny, yes, but rude).

3 noisy earwiggles

3 noisy earwiggles
Like sitting in a row,
Pretending to be football fans,
All shouting, "Earwig go!"

If you come along and say,
 "Raaaah! It is me!
Shall I eat you up?"
They shout, "Hey! Ref-e-reeee!"

If you try to catch them,
Each one runs and hides.
If you lift their flower pot up,
They all shout, "Offsides!"

When you get the giggles,
They run away.
They are just the funniest snacks
You will see all day.

Jelly poem

Jelly in the water.
That looks good!
Pop it in a jam jar,
Save it for my pud.

Forget all about it,
Leave it for a week.
Jelly goes all wiggly.
Tadpoles! Take a peek!

Never mind, I'm hungry,
Pop them in my dish.
Little bit of custard on,
Yum! Dee-lish!

Feel a bit jumpy,
Wonder how come?
Sumwun's done a trick on me,
There's froggies in my tum!

Y mice?

I think mice
Are nice.
They are just
The right size
For pies.

Y deers?

Deers are very nice in pies
But hard to get the crust on.
Because of the hard things on their heads
That sum teeth can get bust on.

(Did you know that saying "deers" is wrong?
Good, because this is a naughty song.
So deers deers deers deers deers deers
deers deers, ect.)

Rabbit rolls

Rabbits are handy,
(Also tastier than moles).
Plus you can catch them easy
And pop them in your rolls.

Not fair snacks

Moles are a bit like bats,
They both need glasses.
Only bats fly 2 high to catch.
Also moles hide in underpasses.
(Boo shame)

Hedgehogs are not fair either

Hedgehogs are not fair either,
All covered in prickles.
Y can't they just have fur on?
Because fur only tickles.

My best snack

My best snack is mooses or pizza.
But which wun I cannot decide.
My dream is to have both together—
A snack that is 6 feet wide.

BEST WOLFIE NURSERY RHYMES

2 little birds

2 little birds sitting on the wall,
Bag me the fat wun, you get the small.

Baa baa black sheep

Baa baa black sheep,
Have you got a sec?
Yes sir, yes sir…
Aren't you a wolf?
Oo heck!

Mary had a little lamb

Mary had a little lamb
Her fleece was very hairy.
The lamb was very tasty,
But not as nice as Mary, har har.

Hickery dickery

Hickery dickery dock,
The mousy had a shock.
The clock struck wunce
I had him for lunch.
Serves him right for running up my clock.

Old Macdonald

Old Macdonald had a farm
Ee–I–ee–arrroooo!
And on that farm, he had sum ducks,
Chew chew chew chew chew.

A rude insect

Ladybug ladybug
Spotty as a mutt.
Spots on her wings and spots on her...
(hem hem, bit rude)

Eek eek

Eek eek Eek Eek Eek Eek Eek

Eek, eek, the mice do skweek,
When they want their mommy.
So do your skweeking practiss,
If you want wun in your tummy.

CRAFTY TRICK POEMS

Hedgehog tricking

Hello Mister Hedgehog,
Can I hold your coat?
Thank you, now you won't get stuck
Halfway down my throat.
(Only kidding, not really)

So there

Smellybreff, Smellybreff,
Fly away home.
The lair is on fire,
Your teddy has gone.

Har har, I tricked you!
Your brane is so small.
That is because of you
Driving *me* up the wall.

Crocodiles are crafty

Crocodiles are Crafty
And I will tell you Y.
If you go to say hello,
They whisper back
good-bye.

Crafty woodworms

Dad said to a woodworm, "Bah!
All you do is chew!"
The woodworm said, "Oh, sorry pal,
Was I boring you?"

Mister Twister

He is very crool and crafty,
Plus a master of dizgizze (cannot spell it).
He will come and be a stealer,
When it's time for beddy-bize.

So if you smell sum pepper
And you are not eating stew,
Be careful, Mister Twister might
Come creeping up on you.

He whispers very softly
And says, "Look into my eyes."
And if you do, he gives you
A big horrible surprise.

Do you like getting splinters?
Do you want to have a blister?
Then maybe you would like to
Have a friend like...
Mister Twister!

My box of tricks

I have got a lot of tricks,
I keep them in a box.
There is an arrow-through-your-head,
Plus a ~~sine~~ sign to trick a fox.

There's a mouse that runs up trousers,
Plus a little wind-up flea.
Plus sum funny itchy powder,
Plus a cushion that goes Whoopee.

There's a rattle with a snake on,
Plus fake caterpillar poo.
There's a little skweezy froggy,
That will do a skwirt on you.

But my best tricks are celery sticks.
You stick 2 up your gums,
And say, "Have you seen the werewolf?
Oh no, look out! Here he comes!"

Dizgizzes (cannot spell it)

It's good dressing up as a granny
To trick small Riding Hoodies.
You get into bed and you say, "Hello Red,
Do you mind if I eat up your goodies?"

It's good dressing up as a sheep,
And tricking Miss Little Bo Peep.
You do a Baa twice, and she goes, "Ah Nice,"
And then you drive off in her jeep.

But it's bad dressing up as a bunny.
I did that just wunce for a dare.
A farmer got hasty, saying,
"Hmm you look tasty,"
And bang went his shotgun—not fair.

POEMS TO MAKE YOU GO "HMMMM?"

Isn't it funny about caterpillars?

1st they eat nettles
That are very very stingy.
Then they go hard and
Then they get wingy.
(Hmmm?)

Ant, wasp, hornet, bee

Ant, wasp, hornet, bee,
Which wun do you like to see?
Best of all,
I like ants,
Because they are the funniest if…
You get them down your pants.

ect.

If you ever get fed up of writing down
"And all that kind of stuff,"
You can say it in a short way,
(3 letters are enuff).

Sum hot shots write down, *etc.*,
Or even *etcetera*.
But I like writing *ect.* best,
So nah nah nah nah nah.

If I was a teecher

If I was a teecher,
I would be very nice.
If somebody said, "Can I go to the bathroom?"
I would say, "Yes, go twice."

If I was a teecher,
I would make math fun.
I would say, "Here is a hard kwestion.
What is wun + wun ?"

If I was a teecher,
I would not give citations.
I'd say, "Well done, you naughty boy,
Have a nice vacation."

If I was a teecher,
I would not say, "Be quiet!"
I would say, "Today, for a change
Let's have a lovely riot."

If I was a teecher,
And it got to half-past 9,
I would say, "Enuff for today.
Buzz off, it's go-home time."

So come on all you teechers,
Do not be strict and crool.
Be noble to your pupils,
Let them muck about in school.

Say boo to blue

If you feel a little blue
And lonely in the night,
Make friends with a line painting gang,
And then you'll be all white.

Sand

Sand is OK
For pits and pies.
But not much good
For ears and eyes.

I like sand
That is underneef
Not on top
Or in your teef.

HANDY POEMS

Stick to glue

Glue is very handy,
When you write a letter.
You could close the envelope with a hammer
  and nails,
But I think glue is better.

My small handy hero

Who is that flitting
Around my house?
A bird, a plane,
Or a Supermouse?
No it is not.
Sorry about that.
It is not a hero,
Only a bat.

But yes he is a hero,
Hip hip hero-eee!
He eats flies and mousteekos, moskeatoes,
  stingy things,
And it keeps them all off me.

Handy poem about not having a tail

To be a wasp or slimy snail,
Would be handy in a way.
OK, somewun might step on you,
But they would not pull your tail, eh?

bandy tricks for when you itch

I will not itch when I get rich.
I will pay 2 chimpanzees
To have a good old feel around
And capture all my fleas.

Also, I will buy myself
A fence post on a spring.
So I just stand there and get scratched,
While the post goes bing bong bing.

bing bong bing

Short handy poem for testing if you
have got a rude habit

Listen to this kwestion and answer it kwick.
What does this remind you of? pick
                              roll
                                flick
(Har har got you, that was a NOSY trick!)

HANDY TIPS FOR SMALL WOLFCUBSITTERS

Tip 1
Toothies

Just because his teeth look small
And his mommy calls him "Love."
Best not hold your finger out.
(Not without a glove,
OK?)

Tip 2
Keep hoping

Have sum handcuffs handy,
Also a piece of rope,
Plus a fire xtingwisher,
And never give up hope.

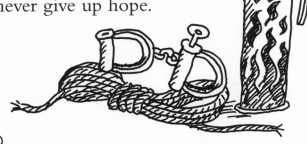

Tip 3
Bouncing your baby cub

Bounce him in the bouncer,
Till he dribbles down his chin.
Bounce bounce bounce,
BOINGGG!
There he goes again.

Bounce him in the bouncer,
Panting like a dog.
Out go his legs like
A flippy floppy frog.

Bounce him in the bouncer,
Till he does his party dance.
Down there, up in the air,
Whoops, no pants.

Bounce him in the bouncer,
Mind the pussy cat!
Bounce bounce bounce bounce,
Meow, squashed flat.

Baby cubs like bouncing,
They like their bounces ruff.
So when he hits the ceiling
You say—TUFF!!

Tip 4
No hard skweezing

Babies are kwite dangerous.
This is what they do.
Wah wah hick burp,
Throw-up puddle poo.

If you give them piggie backs
Or 2 much rabbit stew,
(Remember)
Wah wah hick burp
Throw-up puddle poo.

Tip 5
Do a nice shocking lullaby

1, 2, 3, 9, 8,
Once I ate some Goose Flakes.
4, 7, 9, 8, 10,
But I threw it up again.

Y did you let it go?
Because it made me itch my toe.
Then what did you do?
Bonged its head with my shoe!

Tip 7
Do another shocking lullaby

Rockaby wolfcub,
Up in the tree.
How did you get there?
Was it windee?

Yes it was windee,
Now I am stuck.
Whoops now I've squashed you.
That was tuff luck.

Dear Mom and Dad,

I got your letter today saying yes, your poems are handy, they have stopped the draft under the back door of The Lair. Not fair, just because I was harsh 2 Smells, and he is your darling baby pet.

Anyway, I am doing them all again in a neat book, because Yeller and Normus say they are kwite good, hem hem. Also Stubbs says they are Ark-cellent. Now I will probly sell them and get rich, so try not to get 2 jealous, all right? Also, just in case Dad likes fly poems, I am sending this wun as a P.S. but no more, OK?

Yours arm-achely,

L. Wolf (poet)

74

Flies, what is the point of them?

I do not see the point of flies,
They just go around and around.
Dad hits them with his paper,
And they fall down on the ground.

They buzz against the window.
But if you skwash them flat,
A hundred others come along.
What is the point of that?

They are fond of Uncle Bigbad.
They want to be his friend.
But he is like a horse's tail.
Swish, bonk...

The end.

(Get it?)